Little Gold Star

A SPANISH AMERICAN CINDERELLA TALE

Retold by ROBERT D. SAN SOUCI

Illustrated by SERGIO MARTINEZ

HarperCollins*Publishers*

To my wonderful friends
Debra, Michael, and Nicholas Steele
—R.S.S.

To Carmen, my beloved wife
—S.M.

AUTHOR'S NOTE

This story, well known in New Mexico and the Southwest, is adapted from tales of Spanish origin, though it has roots in such tales as "Cinderella" and narratives collected by the Brothers Grimm and other folklorists.
In addition to working with previously translated versions of the tale from such books as *Literary Folklore of the Hispanic Southwest,* by Aurora Lucero-White Lea, and José Manuel Espinosa's *Spanish Folk-Tales from New Mexico,* published in 1937 as Volume XX of the memoirs of the American Folk-Lore Society, I used new translations of several old Spanish-language texts that were reprinted in the American Folk-Lore Society volume.

Little Gold Star

Text copyright © 2000 by Robert D. San Souci
Illustrations copyright © 2000 by Sergio Martinez

Printed in Singapore at Tien Wah Press.

www.harperchildrens.com

Library of Congress Cataloging-in-Publication Data
San Souci, Robert D.
Little gold star: a Spanish American Cinderella tale /
retold by Robert D. San Souci; illustrated by Sergio Martinez.
p. cm.
Summary: A Spanish American retelling of the familiar story of a kind girl
who is mistreated by her jealous stepmother and stepsisters. In this version,
the Virgin Mary replaces the traditional fairy godmother.
ISBN 0-688-14780-1 (trade)—ISBN 0-688-14781-X (library)
[1. Fairy tales.   2. Folklore—New Mexico.]   I. Martinez, Sergio, ill.
II. Title.   PZ8.S248 Li 2000   398.2'09789—dc21   99-50290

10   9   8   7   6   5   4   3   2   1
❖
First Editon

*I*n what is now New Mexico, there was once a sheepherder named Tomás whose wife had died. He had an only child, Teresa. She kept house while he tended his flocks high in the hills.

Then a widow and her two daughters moved nearby.
The woman visited often, and one day she said to Tomás,
"Surely you are as lonely as I. Marry me, and make us
both happy."

When Tomás refused, the widow began to weep. Not
knowing what to do, Tomás agreed to be married.

Teresa cared little for the haughty woman or her vain
daughters, Inez and Isabel, but she said nothing.

As soon as Tomás's new wife moved into the house,
she made life a misery for him and Teresa. She nagged her
husband so much, he stayed in the hills longer and longer.
And while he was away, Teresa had to do all the chores.

On one rare visit home, Tomás brought his wife and stepdaughters gifts of flowers and oranges. To Teresa he gave a lamb with soft white fleece.

As soon as her husband returned to his flocks, Teresa's stepmother killed the lamb. Handing the heartbroken girl the fleece, she ordered, "Go wash this in the river, so I can make myself a soft pillow."

Teresa had no choice but to obey. As she scrubbed, a fish snatched the wool and swam away. Teresa tried to grab back the fleece but failed. Fearing her stepmother's anger, she began to weep.

Just then, a woman dressed in blue came by and asked, "Why are you crying?"

When Teresa told her, the woman said, "Go up to that little shack on the mountainside. Tend the old man and the child there and sweep the floor, and I will bring the fleece back to you."

Teresa climbed the path to the hut. Inside, an old man with tangled hair and beard dozed while a baby cried in his cradle. Teresa gently rocked the infant and sang a lullaby until he went to sleep. Then she combed the old man's hair and beard. Finally she swept the place clean.

Just as she finished, the woman in blue returned, carrying the snow-white fleece. She gave this to Teresa, saying, "Good child, your kindness carries its own blessing." She touched Teresa's forehead with her finger, and a little gold star appeared there.

Teresa did not know it, but the woman was Blessed Mary. The old man was Saint Joseph, and the baby was the Holy Child, the baby Jesus.

The moment Teresa returned home, her stepmother cried, "Why have you been away so long?"

Teresa told her what had happened, but the woman did not believe her. Then her stepmother tried to scrub off the gold star, but it just shined brighter. And when she touched the fleece, it turned muddy.

The next morning, Isabel was sent to wash the fleece. Again, a fish carried it off, and the woman in blue came. She told the girl to tend the old man and the baby and to take the stewpot off the fire. In return, she would restore the fleece.

But inside the shack, Isabel spanked the Holy Infant because he was crying, pulled Saint Joseph's beard, and dropped the pot, spilling stew all over the floor.

When Blessed Mary returned, she gave Isabel the now-spotless fleece. But as she touched the girl's forehead, she said, "Your unkindness carries its own penance." At this, horns grew out of the sides of Isabel's head.

"What have you done, you silly girl?" her mother asked when she saw Isabel's horns. She tried to twist and tug them off her daughter's head.

"*Ay! Ay! Ay!*" cried the girl.

Her mother pulled harder, but she only made the horns grow longer. She angrily ordered Inez to wash the fleece, because it had become dirtier than ever when the stepmother touched it.

Inez also had the fleece carried off by a fish. She too met the woman in blue, who sent her to care for the old man and the child and to clean the ashes from the fireplace. But Inez scolded the Holy Infant, ignored Saint Joseph, and strewed the hearth ashes all over the floor.

For her punishment, the girl sprouted a pair of donkey's ears.

Yank as she might, Inez's mother only made the ears grow bigger and shaggier. At last she gave up and sewed heavy black *mantillas*, veils, for her daughters to wear.

Because Teresa bore a gold star while her stepsisters wore hideous horns and ears, they taunted her even more. They called her *"Estrellita de Oro,"* "Little Gold Star," turning the words into a cruel joke.

About this time, a fiesta was held in honor of the patron saint of the town. The morning of the festival, Isabel and Inez, dressed in fine satins and high *mantillas,* sat in the front pew at mass with their mother. Near them sat Don Miguel, the handsome young man whose mansion overlooked the plaza.

To one side of the altar knelt Teresa. By chance Miguel noticed her, though Isabel and Inez kept fluttering their fans to draw his attention. At one point Teresa's white veil slipped back, and Miguel saw the star shining on her forehead. But before he could speak to her, Teresa left to return to her chores.

That night Miguel opened his home for feasting and dancing.

Left behind by her stepmother and stepsisters, who went in a carriage, Teresa walked to the party. Her white dress was shabby compared to the elegant gowns that swirled around her, but her gold star outshone the jewels the other women wore.

Seeing the star, Miguel moved through the crowd

toward Teresa. He smiled and bowed, and they began to
dance. As was the custom, the young couple danced
silently and distantly, looking at the floor rather than at
each other.

As they danced, Teresa felt her sadness giving way to
joy. The tenderness she had seen in Miguel's eyes
matched the feeling that was growing in her heart.

Suddenly Teresa's stepmother took her arm and pulled her aside. "You wretched girl," the woman whispered angrily. "How dare you come here and embarrass us? Go home at once!" At these harsh words, Teresa turned and fled.

As the music ended, Miguel finally looked up and discovered his dancing partner was gone. He asked who she was, but because Teresa always kept to herself, no one recognized her. Her stepmother remained silent. Still Miguel vowed to find her, though he did not know her name.

At dawn he rode out, stopping at every house, ranch, and farm to ask about the mysterious young woman. Late in the day he came to Tomás's house.

"*Buenas tardes,*" Teresa's stepmother greeted the young man.

"Good afternoon," he responded, then explained the reason for his visit.

"I don't know this stranger you are seeking," the woman said. "But I invite you to take some refreshment with us."

Miguel politely agreed. Isabel and Inez brought hot chocolate and little cakes Teresa had baked that morning. Each tried to catch Miguel's eye and put herself ahead of her sister.

When Teresa's stepmother had seen Miguel approaching, she had locked Teresa in a small room. Now the girl happened to brush her forehead, touching the gold star as she sighed, "I wish I could see Miguel again."

At the same moment, in the parlor, the housecat mewed, *"Narow, narow."* Then, to everyone's surprise, it said, "Little Gold Star *is* here, right in the house."

"Did you hear that?" Miguel exclaimed. "The cat said she is here!"

"You are hearing things," said Teresa's stepmother, kicking at the cat while her daughters jabbed at it with their fans. But the cat clawed away their *mantillas,* revealing their ears and horns. The young women fled in dismay, with their mother running after them. Then the cat led Don Miguel to Teresa.

"Little Gold Star!" he cried joyously.

"My proper name is Teresa, Señor," she replied.

"Señorita Teresa," he said, "I beg you to marry me."

"I would marry you in an instant," answered Teresa, "but you must ask my stepmother's permission first."

"Of course," Miguel agreed. Then he kissed her hand and left.

The next morning, Miguel's servant brought a letter asking for Teresa's hand in marriage. After she had read it, Teresa's stepmother shook with anger. To Isabel and Inez she said, "I will allow Teresa to marry only if she performs three tasks. So help me to choose some impossible challenges."

When they had agreed upon the tasks, the stepmother went to Teresa and said, "You must do three things before we return from market. If you fail, I will refuse Don Miguel's marriage offer."

"First," said Isabel, "you must fill ten bottles with birds' tears."

"Next," said Inez, "you must stuff twelve mattresses with birds' feathers."

"Finally," said Teresa's stepmother, "you must prepare a tableful of fine food." Then the three left.

Though Teresa despaired of completing these tasks, she was determined to try. But she could find only a handful of rice and beans in the house; not a single bird appeared in the sky.

Suddenly, there was a tap at the door. Blessed Mary stood there. "Do not worry," she said. "Touch your gold star and call the birds of heaven to help."

Teresa did, and instantly the sky was filled with birds. They wept until she filled ten bottles with their tears. The second time she touched her star, the birds shed feathers like soft rain, while Teresa stuffed twelve mattresses. When she touched the star a third time, the birds flew away and came back, carrying delicacies of every sort.

Teresa's stepmother and stepsisters gazed in wonder when they returned. Realizing that Teresa had been blessed, the woman sent Miguel a letter agreeing to the marriage.

Tomás returned in time to see his daughter married. And the joy of the bride and groom touched everyone. Gradually, Teresa's stepmother grew less disagreeable and began to treat her as a daughter. Isabel and Inez grew kinder, and the donkey ears and horns became smaller, then finally disappeared.

Miguel and Teresa lived lovingly all their days. And the little gold star remained a sign of heaven's blessing on them and their children.